For Sungjin
—H.Y.

The illustrations in this book were made with colored pencils.

Library of Congress Control Number 2019936977

ISBN 978-1-4197-4224-8

Text and illustrations copyright © 2020 Hyewon Yum
Book design by Steph Stilwell

Printed and bound in China
10 9 8 7 6 5 4 3 2 1

ABRAMS The Art of Books
195 Broadway, New York, NY 10007
abramsbooks.com

Lion Needs a Haircut

Hyewon Yum

Abrams Books for Young Readers
New York

You need a haircut.

Yes, you do. Don't worry.
Barber Goat will take good care of you.
His scissors won't cut your ears.

I know. I'm not worried.
I just don't want to get a haircut.

Oh, I understand why you don't want to.
But there's nothing to be scared of.
Are you afraid of razors?

I see, I see.
You're thinking you'd
look like an antelope?
You'll just get
a little trim.
No antelope
hair for you!

YOU are GETTING a HAIRCUT.

You look grubby, your mane is wild, and it's extremely hard to brush your hair!

YES!
ROAR!

I just wanted my hair
to look like yours.

Oh, you did?
I thought you were scared.
I used to be scared
of scissors, razors,
and blow dryers
when I was a kid.

I know I look amazing,
but you will be as handsome as me
after you get a little trim.

Stop kissing me.
It's prickly.
You need a haircut!

Me? No. I don't need a haircut.

Yes, you do. Are you scared?

No, why?
I've been to the barbershop
a million times.

Oh, no problem, then.
We can go to the barbershop together.
Mama said you need a haircut, too!

Yes, your hair is wild and unruly!
And she doesn't like how you always
have mustard on your mustache
and breadcrumbs in your beard.

See?
If you get a haircut, I will.

But I look just fine!
Short hair doesn't look
good on me . . .

Alrighty.
No haircut for either of us.
Sounds fair to me.

Wait! Grr. I'll get a haircut. But absolutely no antelope hair. Just a little trim, OK?

Are you sure?

Since you've been to the barbershop a million times, you go first.

You look great, kiddo.

You, too.
See, there was nothing to be worried about.

I wasn't worried.

Yes, you were. But it's OK.
I won't tell anyone.